Smile

by

Olivia King

Dedicated to my brother. Thank you for being you.

Contents

Fundamental realisation

I have no animosity towards you, yet I feel the heat of rage burn in my chest when I catch sight of you, hear your voice, stroke your hair, hug your shoulders, smudge your mascara with my finger tips when you sleep.

I have no hatred towards you, yet I bite down on my fist to stop from screaming profanities when you spin in your clothes and ask me how you look, when you read your amateur poetry at open night, when you smile and ask me to pass you the salt.

That thing you do, stepping deliberately on dried leaves on the pavement, trembling with delight at the sound of the delicate crunch. It amuses you. You turn and shrug. I watch you. Can you determine what I am feeling and thinking?

Then there's the flossing. Every single night you walk all over the apartment with your mouth hanging open pulling the satin thread through your teeth. How did I ever think that was okay? It takes you 30 minutes to do your teeth each night, I've timed it. There's no variation either. You do it for exactly 30 minutes — nothing more or less. It troubles me, yet I don't ask you about it. It angers me these days.

Mondays are now the worst. You stay home. I work in our bedroom. It used to be my sanctuary working from home with just the tall ferns and Bryony for company. Bryony brings me respite and I feel at peace watching her sleep, leap and hearing her purr.

I feel you and I stayed in the same place after meeting. So typical that we met at work. Every single day we stared at each other across the desk. We took the same bus to work. Of course we would get used enough to each other to think we had an attraction.

But, you don't like the time apart, now I no longer sit across from you at work. Or do you just not trust me?

You start working from home on Mondays. 'Samuel? If all goes well, I'll be working full-time from home too!' There's your familiar and increasingly grating shriek of delight and your refusal to call me Sam - my preference. I've only asked you since we first met.

Bryony hides in the corner licking her paws obsessively. With more than one of us at home during the day she is sullen like she is in the evenings. I miss her dainty paws padding softly on my chest while I answer emails.

Sundays have become bad too, now that your parents have moved into the apartment block. You wanted them in the same building. You said, you worry about them otherwise. Now they are an elevator ride away. Perfect.

And, of course, they obliged happily, paying over the odds for the roof terrace. Their favourite child wanted them with her, so nothing was too expensive. And of course, I said nothing. How could I? Did they see me grinding my teeth? Or did they think it was because I put my back out moving their things in? They were stingy about the moving costs after shelling out full whack for the place. I didn't notice that about them when we first started seeing each other, but I guess it explains why I bore the cost of our wedding, honeymoon and apartment. I'm still waiting for them to pay their half for the 300 guest wedding. It didn't bother me so much before, but now, it does.

On Sundays your parents are here for a long lunch. I listen to your father blustering on about his golf and sailing, spitting in my direction as he drowns one cold after another. Your mother, happy with the break from him, tidies up and folds our clothes, commenting on all our things, including my mismatched socks and old boxers.

"Well, think of the money you've saved on a housekeeper. Put it towards some golf lessons!" Your father doesn't stop until late in the afternoon when the drink overtakes him and he lies snoring on the couch. Drooling over the linen white of my throw pillows. Bryony hides under the bed, her green eyes wide and alert, until they leave.

Within a week of your parents moving into the apartment block, you let our housekeeper go - the first muse I've had since you chased away Ben. You blamed your mother of course for raising suspicions in you, but I know better. You've always been excessively jealous. I found your possessiveness attractive, comforting and flattering once. I feel otherwise now. It is clawing and I feel you under my skin even when we are apart.

I shake my head, try to loose myself, turn up the music and start a new article. Bryony dashes across the room and hides between my ankles under the desk. You won't let her be. You breeze in and kneel down, dragging her out, purposefully stroking my leg as you do so and smiling lasciviously. I used to find your efforts at flirting seductive and playful. Now, I pretend not to notice to keep from retching. I thump the keyboard keys harder and harder, as if commanding you to leave me in peace. Instead it arouses you. I forget how easily we are still able to satiate each other. You rub my shoulders and nod towards the bed. I shake my head and stare ahead at the computer screen, hoping you just leave. But you don't. You straddle me instead, knocking my papers on the floor and by the time we break apart it is already noon. You shake your blonde curls, throwing your head back, releasing me once more into my private shell.

I can actually tell you when it started. When you rushed Ben out of my life. He was a friend, confidant and muse. We had a lot in common. I still ache for his words and thoughts. Nothing I have worked on has come close to what I used to produce. Things have not been the same since. Why were you so spiteful? So petty? Can I not have anything of my own? Just for me? Must you have it all? I watch you throw on a robe. You give me a light, lingering kiss, eyeing me closely. "Lunch?", you ask.

I huddle under the full force of a power shower. As hot as possible, hoping the steam clears my pores of you. I cry. I am louder than I expect. Shaking with uncontrolled sobs, my throat aches. I scrub at my skin harder and harder.

I am startled by the sound of scratching. It is Bryony waiting at the shower door. This has become our ritual too. She and I under the hot steam. It's something new for her. I leave the door ajar. I'll be awhile.

I want you to forgive me. I want to tell you about how I feel and why I want to leave. But I want forgiveness. I can't leave without it.

I eat my tuna sandwich. You make good lunches. But knowing it is made by you? I push half of it away. You look up from your magazine and grin "We could make a day of it. I'm not getting much done."

I shake my head, "They need my copy by noon tomorrow."

"Oh I see," you mouth exaggeratedly, rolling your eyes and smiling conspiratorially at Bryony. She ignores you, continues to rest on the towel on the floor. You don't ask about her new found love for regular showers. I wonder if you care. I take in the green fleck of lettuce sticking out of your side tooth and decide not to tell you it's there. You'll floss it out later right?

I resent your carefree take on where we are. How can you remain so calm? You barely raise an eyebrow at anything I say or do. You are as impassive and personable as when we met. I used to find it relaxing. It used to be pleasant to be with someone who was just there. Now it is an irritant. Because you are always there. In my belongings, in my work, in my thoughts, in my scent, just everywhere, all over me, stuck like heavy tar building up for the next 10 years. I even hate the way you look at Bryony. Like you are now. You take tiny bites a mange tout while observing her clean herself. Can she not have some privacy either! I shake my head, try to stop the red of fury threatening to swallow me whole. I push my chair back and take the plate to the sink. I wash it cautiously and carefully. Breathing in and out. Focussing on the sound of running water. Counting to six and back again. It helps that Bryony sits on the counter watching me.

"Of course, I will always love Samuel. So gentle, kind and thoughtful. But I knew something was wrong. I think it was the way he washed his plate. I mean, I had seen him do the plates! Even dry them on a couple of occasions! But marriage, it can be such a fickle dance, with so few breaths in between and so little room to just twirl away for a while when you need to. That was why I had to leave, even though he begged me not to. I left Bryony with him and came upstairs to my parents. They were worried of course. I just didn't feel safe to be in that flat with him. He didn't even finish the tuna sandwich I made him. There was certainly something amiss. So of course I came to my parents and planned to stay with them. Then, to hear that alarm go off like that in the middle of the night. It woke us all. The stench in the hallway is just awful now. I mean our whole flat and all our things up in flames! Are you sure it was him? Poor Samuel!"

"I'm not sure what you mean, ma'am. We didn't find anybody in the flat," says the fire marshal.

"Well, what about a cat. Did you find that?"

"No, nothing."

"Well, I just don't understand! Wasn't it an accident?"

The fire marshal shuffles his feet, "Now tell me again the last time you saw your husband."

I really didn't mean for any of this to happen. But when I returned to the apartment block and saw the fire engines I just decided to walk away. I knew you would find a way to blame me.

When you left for her parents I was overjoyed. I helped you pack. Once gone, I decided to pack the rest of your things. Then I took a long bath by candlelight. Then it happened. An idea burst into life in my mind, took over every cell in my body and I started to write with renewed purposefulness. I stepped out to pick up some supplies from the 24 hour store and must have forgotten to shut the door. Bryony came after me and when we returned there were fire engines everywhere.
I walked away with Bryony in my arms.
It was meant to be, I told myself.

So here I am two months later. It turns out that Bryony is my muse. And she will never leave me or criticise me and I don't find anything about her even the slightest bit annoying. I never heard from you. I guess, sometimes things really do just work out.

Interlude in Paris

"Isabelle, please be careful with her. Portia Nols fired the last three translators and I have run out of ideas," says Stanley Owen, resting his attache case on the marble table and gesturing to a waiter. He straightens his tie and glances round before taking a seat.

He is nervous, she thinks, otherwise he would not have called her Isabelle - she dislikes the formality of it, preferring to be known as Izzy. Apart from that, he looks well. The last time they met, Stanley was in London finalising his divorce. He was pale, withdrawn and jittery when he spoke. Izzy smiles, glad Paris had brought Stanley back to his old self. She even noticed a weightlessness to his step when he arrived at the cafe. Gone was sluggish Stanley, with the perpetual frown and eye tic. Or perhaps her recollection is an exaggeration. She can't be sure. Izzy is someone who is considered a more unreliable witness than your average person. She notices all the good things about people, all the positives, and ignores the alarm bells, red flags and registers none of the dire fault lines. It has been this way for most of her life.

Izzy arrived in Paris two days ago and settled into her short term let. This is only her second time in the city, and she is hoping to make the most of it. After all, expenses are covered by Stanley's publishing house and there is nothing stopping her from taking in the sights and enjoying the city while she is here. Her mind is cluttered with snapshots of all the iconic movies, books and photography of the city. She hasn't captured any of the downside to the European city or the fact that she will have to spend the majority of her time working. She knows she needs to focus on the task at hand. This is an important assignment, one that she knows many would have wanted. Yet, here she is wondering about which museum to visit later today and what cafe to sit at to people watch. With Izzy, temptation is sure to win out.

"You look fantastic Stanley!" says Izzy.

Stanley blushes and nods, his blonde hair falling into his eyes. "I love it here. I am having a wonderful time. I'm hoping they offer me a permanent role."

"Wow! That is wonderful. And thank you for thinking of me. It's a magnificent opportunity. I didn't even realise Portia Nols lived here."

"Oh yes? There have been a few pieces about her in the local press. Not much in the way of detail. Her last two books are still doing really well. And being the person who discovered her, well you can imagine how good it looks for me!" Stanley is clearly pleased with himself.

Izzy laughs happily. This is just what she needs. Finally, an opportunity to work with a best selling author who most know nothing about. This surely signals a route somewhere up the ladder. She is sure of it. She realises this could finally be the break she needs to work as a translator on major novels. She reflects on her early years in publishing and realises how much she has enjoyed the journey but she never imagined she would come this close to success. She never doubted her career choice and persisted even when others told her to do something else. Well, that is standard practise. It really is, especially in publishing.

When Izzy met Stanley, he was a junior editor trying to make a name for himself while navigating the idiocies of a failing marriage. Izzy had been drawn to him instantly. Somehow she knew he would make it, and get there fast. She did all she could to stay in his circle of acquaintances hoping it would eventually pay off.

"Are you seeing anyone these days?" Izzy asks.

Stanley shakes his head, "Nothing serious. The dating scene in Paris offers up choices I never thought I would have and I am not keen to settle down again any time soon. I have made too many friends, if you can ever have too many. I still think of Matt of course ... but I have moved on."

Izzy doesn't want to hear about Stanley's sad divorce. She wants to selfishly retain her positive outlook on her experience in Paris.

"I've been doing a bit of dating," she says largely to herself. Of course, she hadn't been, but she didn't know what else to say to establish familiarity with Stanley. Izzy stops herself from continuing, realising that Stanley is scanning the people in the cafe, and also hadn't asked her to elaborate further. She observes him check his watch twice and slurp down the last of his Americano. He stands and smooths down his linen jacket, pushing his hair from his eyes. "Okay! Get your things. Its time to meet her!"

Portia Nols stares out the ornate sash window, cradling her cat Octavia. She strokes Octavia gently, and speaks in hushed tones while watching pedestrians walk hurriedly towards the metro. It is her morning ritual to spend an hour loosing herself in the people out there, watching them closely and thinking about what their lives are like. Her daily ritual has stayed the same since she moved to Paris. In the afternoons she dictates some of her thoughts into a recorder and hands them over to her assistant to type up. The method of working suits her and she hates to be distracted from it.

Octavia spends that full hour in the mornings in Portia's arms, peering out the window. She is used to their daily routine, but is never satisfied with it. She has always found Portia to have uncomfortable arms, all angles with little padding. It isn't so bad in the winter months, Portia always wears many layers, but in the summer, it is different, the bare bony arms pushing against her soft coat, and Octavia prefers softness.

Portia is nervous today, which makes her twitch and tremble, increasing Octavia's discomfort. She is concerned that her publisher will send her yet another obsequious, self-involved translator. She is tired at having to convey her vision to those who have so little understanding of what it cost to write the type of book she has. People expect her to be a light touch just because she is in her late 20s. To them she has struck it lucky. They don't know she started writing her book when she was 5. It had grown as she had until she had no choice but to let it go before it consumed all of her.

After her novel was published she adopted Octavia and moved to Paris, leaving her past behind, she hoped forever. She hadn't counted on her obsession with her book returning in full-force when the publisher wanted to translate it. Of course she was pleased. If a story was well-regarded, and she knew hers was, then as many people as possible should read it. She didn't care about the critics. She just wanted her readership to grow.

Since the book was published, the letters had kept coming in. She looked forward to them, learning about other lives, thrilled that people were sharing their deepest thoughts with her. Some days she wasn't even sure which was more important to her — the next manuscript or the letters. But she didn't really care. What difference did it make. She didn't need to overthink it. She had a good life and as far as she was concerned that's all that mattered.

She didn't respond to any of the letters from her readers, she just kept them in a filing cabinet in the study. Her assistant itemised them for her by subject area and date and when Portia wanted to she would just go back to them for more insight into her readers.

Stanley enters first, with Izzy close behind. Portia hears her assistant show the visitors to the couch and offer them refreshments. She strokes Octavia who by now has turned her head and stretched out, lying upside down so she can see the visitors.

"You look well Portia" says Stanley, clasping his hands together and setting his briefcase to the side. Portia nods sits opposite her visitors on another couch. Stanley rests back, his legs crossed. Izzy is perched at the edge of the couch, her notebook open, she has her pen on the ready. She smiles easily, hiding her rising anxiety at meeting the famous author. Octavia hops off Portia's lap and pads over to Izzy, hopping up on the couch and resting against her knee. She sits beside Izzy, fluffy tail bent into a question mark, observing her closely.

"I've never seen her do that before!" says Portia. "Come back here Octavia. Right now!"

Octavia ignores her, fixing her gaze on Izzy. She stretches her front legs and slowly moves into position, sitting squarely on Izzy's lap, purring loudly.

"Well, she's certainly made her decision!" Stanley laughs, "If only all our meetings were this easy."

Portia watches as her assistant brings in the coffee and leaves it on the table, hurrying off.

Izzy is enchanted by the cat. Her anxiety falls away. Her breathing becomes slow and restful. She takes in the sleek fur and the perfectly proportioned ears and most of all Octavia's beautiful eyes. She puts down her notebook and relaxes into Octavia's gaze.

Portia's petite face scrunches up, her green eyes pointed like darts, her arms crossed, she rocks in her seat. She pats her bony lap, then the space next to her on the couch and finally raps her fingers on the coffee table. "Octavia! Octavia!" she calls.

"Erm, perhaps Octavia should be encouraged to go back to Portia now," says Stanley, reaching to lift the cat off Izzy's lap only to receive a sharp scratch, followed by several thumps from her paw and a low growl.

"Octavia," cries Portia, "come here at once." The cat looks at her nonchalantly, and turns back to face Izzy. She nuzzles Izzy's chin and purrs even more loudly.

Izzy smiles apologetically, "Shall we talk about your novel? I'm sure Octavia will get bored of me soon?" She strokes Octavia's soft coat, hoping otherwise. She wants the couch to swallow them both, taking her and Octavia to a place of solitude

21

where they can be together. Octavia has made Izzy feel rested, relaxed and recharged all at once.

Portia reigns in her temper. "Very well. So you are the latest offer from Stanley? I've looked at your previous work and spoken to some of the people you have worked with. I think we'll get along just fine."

Stanley chokes on his coffee genuinely surprised by Portia's decisiveness. He looks from Portia to Izzy and then shrugs. He is relieved. "Well, that's that then. I'll leave the two of you to work out a schedule, shall I?"

Izzy spends the rest of the day with Portia. She feels disconnected, only partly listening to the author, nodding now and again, all the while her thoughts elsewhere. Octavia remains by Izzy, stretching, rolling over and following her when she goes for a walk in the garden. She sits on Izzy's lap for lunch and ignores Portia's pleas to come back to her. She turns her nose up at her favourite treats. When it comes time for Izzy to leave, Octavia paces at the door, tries to follow her out and then sulks for the rest of the evening, refusing to move even for bed.

Izzy wakes early the next morning. She has a week before seeing Portia again. She needs to get a working draft to her by then. She lays in bed with a coffee, but can't bring herself to switch on her computer and start her task. She is excited and happy.

She jumps up and down on her bed (she has always wanted to), falling down laughing and giving herself a big knee hug. The book is very far from her thoughts. She reflects on her career, her journey to becoming a regular in publishing circles, but never quite reaching the pinnacle of her field. She thinks about her life and how she has lived it, always minding everyone else and being careful not to overstep boundaries. She wonders about Paris and all the things she is going to get to see. Then, it suddenly comes to her, she knows what she has to do. It feels like she has no other choice. Without doing this she will never get to the next step of learning who she is. Izzy has always been an avid reader of self-help books and it has all sunk in. In this one moment she decides it just simply has to be, she needs to move and move fast. She selects a white long sleeve t-shirt with black buttons running down the side and pulls on her favourite pair of jeans. She packs the rest of her clothes in her bag and collected her things. She clears the apartment, returns the keys and sets off for the metro, arriving at Portia's an hour later in a rental car. She squeezes the two door into a spot a few feet opposite the entrance of the house. She checks her face in the mirror, putting on some lipstick and light blue eye shadow. She tweaks her cheeks, giving it some colour. She pulls her hair up and away from her face, tying it loosely in a pony tail.

Checking her reflection one last time, she steps out into the pavement and takes in two sharp breaths.

It is a warm day with a light breeze. People walk past her hurriedly, juggling their phones, bags and coffee cups. She smiles, pulling her small handbag up on her shoulder, then locking the car. She sprints across the road and rings the bell to the house. The assistant answers the door. She looks confused, but Izzy pushes past her "I simply must speak to Portia. It's quite urgent."

Portia is at her usual spot by the window, Octavia lying in her arms. When the cat sees Izzy, she wriggles and tries to kick her way out of Portia's arms. But Portia is fast, and holds on to her.

"I can't hide it in any longer," says Izzy, "come away with me Portia! Let's just go on an adventure, just you and me." Izzy is breathless, her voice easy and light. Her smile wide and encouraging. She watches Portia continue to struggle with Octavia.

"What are you talking about?" asks Portia.

"Don't you see? We are meant to be together. Can't you feel it? It was overwhelming me yesterday," says Izzy moving towards Portia and touching her lightly on the shoulder. As Izzy predicted, Portia recoils from her touch. Octavia takes the opportunity to leap into Izzy's waiting arms.

"Are you quite mad? This is intolerable! First they send me a translator who couldn't put a menu together in French, then they send me one who spoke incessantly about how I had misinterpreted my own writing and now this! How dare you come into my home and behave this way?" Portia pushes her hair back and huffs.

"Give her back to me at once!" she says, watching Izzy cuddle the purring Octavia.

Portia's assistant appears at the doorway. "Call the police at once and fetch me something, I am feeling quite faint," says Portia.

Izzy runs for the door, Octavia in her arms. She pushes past the assistant, ignores Portia's yells and crosses the road. Izzy gets into the car and hurriedly puts Octavia on the passenger seat. She puts the car in gear and pushed her way into the traffic. She looks in her rearview mirror. Portia and her assistant are standing at the door looking perplexed. They point in the direction of the car, yelling.

Octavia purrs and moves onto Izzy's lap, looking out the window to the side. They speed off together, both comforted that they have finally found home.

Charters. Mec
marina, at first light.
Lewis had some urban a
perience. "When I was a ki
little El Toro," he said. "Like
foot sailboat. I lived in Strawt
as joy unbound – has always been evident,
perhaps because of her own profound
bereavement, following the death of her
father in 2008, when she was just 19.
Certainly, the shared experience of loss
– which is inevitably woven into the blessing
of love, throughout our lives – is an inherent
element of being human. If we had never
loved, we would never feel loss; and without
an understanding of heartbreak, we might
be unable to show real compassion towards
others. Similarly, could happiness be as great
THE SCIENTIST
Without a properly randomiz
directly comparing the experien
the tractors with their experien
the day they were treated with the
served as a kind of control grou
So what happens now at the library, pick a book, copy out the contents and transp
the first person stealing Dickens and Don Quixote re-purposing porn
pulp fiction to her own ends. She only got threatened with legal
Generally job-avoidant, she worked in the early 1970s in a live sex show
in Times Square, and later as a stripper on the West Coast. Sex was
aretha Reichardt, remembered
painted wooden toys; and Luc
has only recently received credi
graphs documenting the Bauhau
during which they were wrong
her husband. In some cases, the
women survives in the form
manufactured today, notably th
Marianne Brandt's striking
tea sets, put back into produc
after her death in 1983. 'If your co
been vital there will always be so
up where you left off, and that w
to immortality,' Gropius once to
century after the foundation
a female cohort is finally provi
into two suitcases, so they furnished their lodgings
bought for a pound each.
my father worked, my mother made it her mission
her love of literature, music and the arts. We read
Orwell's Animal Farm and Roger Lancelyn Green's
Greek Heroes together; I learnt piano from the age of
by six, declared Beethoven's Für Elise my favourite
enrolled me into the National Children's Orchestra
I would recite the capitals and currencies of all
well as my times tables forwards and backwards
intervention itself you
effect. In the tech worl
page layout or a new p
the usual term is 'A/B
the objective is the same:
basis for comparison.
studies tell you whether

My dog is an anarchist

Violet Shaw was convinced her dog was an anarchist. Not in a past life, no, she meant now.

Stewart was a puppy when he found his way to Violet Shaw's cottage. Violet had been brought up by her grandmother and had lived there all her life. She had never had a pet. Her grandmother was very assiduous about cleanliness and always considered animals to be less than adequate for her household. It was a month after her grandmother passed, that Stewart appeared on Violet's doorstep. His brown fur was matted with mud and debris. She cleaned him up in her kitchen sink, lay him in the basket of her bicycle and went to a local animal sanctuary. They were full up and explained to Violet that perhaps she could consider making an adoption. Violet stared into Stewarts brown eyes and smiled nervously. She left the sanctuary with a starter pack of food and leaflets about caring for a dog.

As a puppy, Stewart spent time with other dogs and cats on his walks, and shared his food when strays came to the door. He spent hours in the small garden to the front of the cottage, watching squirrels and birds. In many respects he was like any other dog. Living his life to the full by going on runs, napping, playing ball and being a constant companion.

Violet became suspicious of Stewart's political leanings when he turned two. They were on a walk in the local park when two of the wealthier residents of the village stopped to pet him. He turned his nose up at them and walked away. It was the first time he had ever done something like that. He was usually welcoming of everyone. When he was approached by the local police officer, Sergeant Jessop, he looked at the man side ways, let out a deep sigh, huffed and walked away, deliberately avoiding all contact.

Violet was quite alarmed and began making note of Stewart's reaction to different people. He had no qualms sitting and listening to the stories told by Lee Oche, a retired school teacher and local environmentalist. He sat at the feet of Ester Amberstone a young musician who used to busk near the village hall on Sundays. And, he spent a lot of time with Fred Young, who set up a co-op for distributing unwanted food. In fact, the more she thought about it, the more Violet blamed Fred for Stewart's behaviour. It was right about the time Fred arrived in the village that Stewart had begun to take offence to the presence of some people. He must have picked up on some of Fred's theories, thought Violet. She knew that Stewart looked forward to seeing Fred when he delivered fruit and vegetables to Violet. Stewart would sit and wag his tail at least fifteen minutes before Fred arrived.

Villagers who participated in the co-op sent their unwanted fruit and vegetables to Fred and he redistributed it to those in need and also to locals who may have wanted something else instead. His scheme was popular, especially with those on low wages and he had even begun to help out some town residents. Stewart often accompanied Fred on his deliveries. At first Violet was happy with the arrangement, she knew how much Stewart liked his walks, and she wasn't always able to take him out as often as she liked. But now she began to reconsider.

It was a clear morning when Violet took Stewart for his Sunday walk. There was a nip in the air and Stewart was wearing his felt green coat. The two went down the main route to the park. They passed Lawrence Cleaver the Second who owned most of the properties in the village and rented them out all year round. He had a copy of the Telegraph newspaper tucked under his arm. He lifted his hat and nodded to Violet. Stewart pulled at his lead, lunged forward and stood in his path. He gave a low determined growl. Even at two years, Stewart was a presence, especially when he barred his teeth, but he was still small. Well, Lawrence Cleaver was very gracious in not getting upset. It was surprising. It was likely he was happy with his financial returns, otherwise he may have caused a scene. Violet reprimanded Stewart immediately, speaking to him in a firm tone. She told Lawrence that Stewart must have been startled by something. Lawrence simply nodded and walked on, grateful he didn't need to stop for a prolonged conversation with one of the villagers.

When they returned to the cottage, Violet paced the living room, asking Stewart why he had behaved that way to Arthur Wainwright. Stewart turned his head away from her and refused to meet her eye. He rejected his afternoon treat and sulked late into the evening.

When Fred arrived with some tomatoes and half a loaf of bread the next morning, Stewart perked up, jumping up to greet him, licking his face and barking with joy. Violet took the opportunity to invite Fred in for some tea. She really did want to get to the bottom of it all. She wanted her suspicions put to rest. She needed to know if her dog was an anarchist. It was best to know. He was only two, and she imagined that as he matured he may take a stronger stance and go beyond growling. His beliefs may even solidify and who knew what that would lead to. Was it Telegraph readers she should add to her avoid list? What about those who read the Daily Mail? Violet furrowed her brow, her anxiety rising.

Fred welcomed the opportunity to chat with Violet. He considered her a friend and unlike most other residents in the village, she always had time for him. They sat in the small living room cupping huge mugs of tea. Both were wearing fingerless gloves, it was still cold this time of year. The tea was very warming. It was Violet's special, thick and frothy. She also laid out an assortment of oddly shaped cookies to share. Fred couldn't be sure of what they were meant to be, but they tasted good. Stewart sat between them, happily gnawing a cookie she had made specially for him.

Violet was someone who did not do small talk. She was never taught to, or encouraged to value it either. So, she asked, "Fred, do you think Stewart is an anarchist?"

Fred stopped mid-sip and moved his mug away from his lips. "What makes you think Stewart is an anarchist Violet?"

"Well, he growled at Lawrence Cleaver yesterday and he runs when he sees Sergeant Jessop. I have been keeping a list of people he seems to have a problem with." Violet paused to watch Fred's reaction. She made it really obvious that she was trying to gauge his thoughts, and even shifted to the front of her chair, to look at him more closely. It is unclear if she meant to make it so obvious. Fred maintained a blank expression, and Violet became agitated, imagining that she had offended him somehow. So she said, "But it's not all bad Fred, he shares his food with the dogs, cats and even some squirrels that come by."

Fred sat back in the wing back chair. He had heard that when Violet lost her grandmother no one had reached out to her. The thing about Violet was that even when she was young, people felt there was something about her that demanded their pity and so they did not enjoy interacting with her. Fred had kept away for other reasons. When he moved to the village, he had been booted out of university. Caught swearing at lecturers and even the dean, he had arranged several sit-its to get the university to decolonise the curriculum for his social policy course. Thing is, even though a lot of students agreed with him, and supported him online, it was harder to get them to turn up for meetings and sit-ins. Anyway, Fred got the official letter telling him to leave, and security escorted him out of student housing. Fred walked as far as he could, unable to hitch a lift, he stopped at the nearest village to catch his breath, pitched a tent on the corner of (what he thought) was an abandoned piece of land, and remained there. Depressed and unable to think through his next course of action, he lay in his tent for several days.

Because the land was actually the back garden of Lee Oche's (retired schoolteacher) cottage, when Lee found him, he allowed Stewart to stay in exchange for light gardening and upkeep to the property. That said, most of the villagers were unhappy about it. There were strict rules on tents and non-residents. Lawrence Cleaver put in a complaint with the local council. Lee Oche stood by his new friend, and put in planning permission for an outhouse. It eventually came through and once built, Fred lived in it and set up his food co-op.

Fred gazed at Violet. He wasn't sure how to handle the situation. He didn't know if dogs could absorb political ideology from those they spent time with. If they could, would they choose one political ideology over another based on the preference of their owner or would they act independently? Fred scratched his head. He needed to help. He could see how concerned Violet was. "Violet, you could train Stewart? It may stop him from growling at people."

"Fred, I think Stewart has been influenced by spending time with you. I really think that's the case."

Fred flushed. "Perhaps you should let Stewart spend time with Lawrence Cleaver to balance things out. That way he can choose which political ideology to follow!" Fred regretted his words immediately.

Violet considered whether Fred had a point there. But decided that she didn't like the thought of anyone spending time with Lawrence Cleaver, let alone Stewart. "More tea?" she asked.

"I can help Violet. I can train Stewart so he keeps his political beliefs, whatever they may be, to himself while on walks around the village. That way he won't growl or attack someone he disagrees with and he can be himself at home."

Violet smiled. Here was the solution! She took Fred up on the offer.

It was the first week of spring. It was sunny with a faint breeze. Stewart was wearing his black coat with red buttons. Violet had heard him cough that morning and was concerned he was coming down with something. She had stitched the coat for him and was very proud of it. He wore it on walks and on colder evenings.

Stewart sat in the garden watching the squirrels eat peanuts and Fred plant seedlings at the front of the cottage. He wanted to help but thought better of it. Fred hoped for a good crop. He and Violet had taken to using as much of the space in her garden to grow different vegetables. Violet sat at the garden table putting the finishing touches to some placards. Lee Oche sat with her, sipping some tea. They were campaigning to convert disused properties into affordable housing. They had started to gain support from people in the town and there were even residents in the village who had become interested. Who knew what they could achieve?

Stewart barked suddenly, startling the others. It was Sergeant Jessop. He paused to look over the low fence. He wasn't happy about the possibility of protests or even campaigns in the quiet village and had begun to make it a point to pass by Violet's cottage every morning. He made copious notes that he was sure central office would need. These things always spiralled out of hand. Jessop knew first hand. Every time he went to one of these protests or gatherings, something happened. It never struck Jessop that it might have something to do with him. But that is a whole other discussion entirely. For now, Violet looked up from her placard and nodded. In the past she would have made some excuse for Stewart's behaviour. Perhaps even offered the Sergeant a biscuit and offer Stewart's morning cough as a way of explaining away his rude bark. But that wasn't what she did. The Sergeant took a leaflet from the pile at the front of the fence, read over it and then looked over at Violet again. He rolled his eyes and put the leaflet in his pocket, walking away. He would check on them again tomorrow.

Fill my soul with heart emojis

There was an emptiness in Dylan. He thought he was unique in feeling this way and felt he needed to do something about it, to somehow mend what he thought was broken.

He stared at the computer screen, feet firmly placed on the floor. He would need to do this or he would loose his nerve. Annie had told him to just act, just do it, take that leap. She had reminded him every day this week. She was fed up of hearing his complaints, as were his other friends. Annie had better things to do. Much as she loved Dylan, she had grown tired of his relentless whining. It had begun to drag her down and even caused her to argue with her husband, Martin. Almost unheard of! The last time they disagreed so passionately about something Martin still had a full head of hair, and she could get away with just one layer of concealer. Annie was comfortable with her solid, predictable relationship with her husband. Their argument rocked her sensitivities and she certainly wasn't going to let that happen again.

Dylan clicked on the link, entered his email address and chose a password. This was it. He filled in details — his likes, dislikes and what he was looking for, added a blurry profile picture and hit save. He let out a loud sigh and reminded himself to breathe. In for seven, hold for four, and out for seven. Or was it eight? He couldn't remember, but followed that pattern of breathing anyway. He stared at the picture. He would update it tomorrow. For now it would do. It didn't show his full face, just his bare torso and chin, and one flexed arm. He liked it. It was taken five years ago. But what of it? Let's see what happens he thought.

Imagine a world where someone like Dylan actually connects with and meets the person of his dreams within 24 hours of loading up a profile on a dating site. Dylan is 42 years of age, he has no children, has never been married, and other than an addiction to caffeine, does not have any vices. Well, he doesn't. He works out everyday, has a full head of straw blonde hair, is over 6 foot, with crystal blue eyes. He has no pets and keeps entertained with the usual cultural and sporting pursuits. So why has it been a problem for Dylan to meet that special someone and form a bond of everlasting love. This was what Annie had asked herself, during the first few months of getting to know Dylan - her colleague, and then boss. Dylan had been promoted very quickly after joining the firm — he was considered sharp and reliable, dependable and supportive. A classic all-round good guy who delivered results. Women and men flirted with Dylan regularly. He was never tempted, but he was always touched by the attention. With everyone he met, there was always something that he felt was not quite right, and when he was a teenager, he told himself he would only start something with someone who felt like the one on sight. It's true. It isn't a lie. This was actually Dylan's take on love and relationships. Oh, he had had a few lovers, but it was simply to explore his sexual desires and attractions. He did what most youngsters do, especially on leaving home for college. After graduating, he quickly joined the workforce and never looked back. Always hoping to meet the one, he never did and the hole in his chest just grew and expanded until he could no longer ignore it. He woke in the middle of the night feeling the weight of it. He felt an inner yank when he observed couples kissing in the street. And he felt it most on his birthday, the holidays and when colleagues spoke about their husbands, wives, fiancés, lovers, dates and crushes at every single opportunity. He was used to that look from others, pity mixed with relief that it wasn't them. Well, that's how he perceived it anyway. Truth be told, some people actually envied Dylan's single status. But he never noticed them. He just picked up on the looks of embarrassment and pity.

A message alert pinged on Dylan's screen. He had received ten likes and there were two messages. One from a person offering to meet him that night for a drink and hook up. The other from someone who wanted to know how often he worked out. Dylan sent Annie a text. 'I've taken the leap xx'.

Annie was in bed with Martin when the text came through. Martin was reading an online blog about DIY hacks in preparation for his week of leave. Annie was scrolling through pictures of celebrities before and after cosmetic surgery. She looked over at Martin and said, "Dylan has finally put a profile up."

Martin paused, looked up from the screen, gave a grunt and went back to his blog.

It wasn't that Martin had done something he wouldn't ordinarily do. It was his standard response to most things Annie said. It was how they communicated. But that night, something in Annie just snapped. It was quite a shock really. Even Annie didn't understand what happened. But she came to a decision and deep down she knew she wasn't going to change her mind. She got up and went to the kitchen. Made herself a hot chocolate and sent Dylan a text asking him the name of the dating site.

By the end of the second week on the dating site, Dylan had been on four dates, with different people. He didn't like any of them on sight, but he decided not to quit. He never gave up at his job, why should he cave in so easily when it came to his personal life? Wasn't it important too? The truth though, which Dylan couldn't admit to himself, was that the hole in his chest, had slowly been eating away at his ideal of love at first sight. But, it would be best not to point that out to him.

Dylan had the full support of Annie, she even helped him purchase new outfits for his dates. She had a keen eye for the latest fashion. Dylan was pleasantly surprised that she had started spending time with him again. He guessed that he was more upbeat these days and less withdrawn. Others at work had noticed it too. There were unforeseen benefits to his search for love.

Annie on the other hand seemed to have become less happy, even though Martin had made good on his DIY promises and fixed the cabinets in the kitchen, painted the bathroom and installed a new shower. It didn't seem to matter to Annie anymore. She was distracted and only really came to life when she spoke to Dylan about his pursuit of love — real love, not the fake kind. That was her new phrase 'real love, not the fake kind.' Dylan never thought to pause and ask her what she meant exactly. And really, that was for the best, because it is unlikely that Annie would have provided a coherent answer. It may have been something she felt, but simply could not explain. Of course, it hadn't stopped her from putting up her own dating profile on websites (other than the one used by Dylan) with the tagline 'looking for real love, not the fake kind.' In her profile picture she held a glass of wine, and stood proudly next to her new kitchen cabinets.

It was on Dylan's seventh date that things changed. The woman who showed up to meet him looked nothing like her profile picture. Her name was Susie and she said she preferred the element of surprise. So instead of being 5 foot 4 inches as she said in her profile, she was 5 foot 7 inches. She wasn't a blonde, she had long auburn curls. She had freckles on the bridge of her nose and green eyes (not brown). Dylan fell in love with her on sight and it didn't seem to matter what she said. They spent the next week wrapped up in each other - calls, texts, emails and dates. Dylan put in for a week of emergency leave, which meant Annie had to cover a lot of his meetings at short notice. Yes, she was happy for him, but she was also jealous - and this took her by surprise. Because it wasn't the type of jealousy that we all occasionally have even for loved ones who have better luck than us sometimes, it was the type of jealousy that ate at your core and triggered a well spring of rage. While Dylan was away, she spoke to the president of the company and swayed the fickle leader's mind to her benefit. He agreed to elevate her position to that of Dylan's equal and give her his most cherished clients. Next she paid a professional to take photos of her and uploaded them to her dating profiles. She also booked an appointment with a cosmetic surgeon. When she went home that night, she ordered a take away just for herself, which caused Martin considerable distress.

When Dylan returned to work, he had a gold wedding band on his finger, and a permanent grin on his face. The fact that he had effectively been demoted didn't bother him. He had married Susie, she would be moving in with him in after moving out of her apartment and finding a new job near him. Annie was away when Dylan returned, in part because she couldn't bear to face him, or for him to pick up on any of her jealousy (which to be fair had just grown in intensity) and also she was abroad recovering in a clinic from cosmetic surgery. She would be away from work for a month. This didn't concern the president of the company, since Annie agreed to work remotely and keep the camera off to attend online meetings.

It was around this time that Martin had his second stretch of leave and decided to do more around the house. He wanted to add a conservatory to the back of the house so Annie could spend time reading and relaxing in there. It was something he had been promising her for over 5 years, right about the time they moved into the house. He felt this would go some way to mending any unhappiness she clearly seemed to have with him. On the first day of setting about the task, Martin was joined by two of his brothers, one of whom had always disliked Martin, for no other reason than he was the youngest in the family and almost always got away with the worst behaviour and not doing anything round the house. Now, this is often mentioned in research about siblings and their position in families, but in Martin's case, it really was true. As the youngest, he was cut a lot of slack. So, when they had a break for afternoon lunch, Martin's eldest brother, who never closed the door to dalliances even though he had been married for 20 years, chanced upon Annie's profile on one dating site, then another and a third. All of a sudden all the pent up anger and years of unhappiness he had with Martin dissolved. A huge weight lifted from his chest, and he felt his jaw unclench. For a moment he thought he was having a stroke and clutched his chest. When nothing else happened, he shrugged, sat back on the chair, cracked open another can of beer and smiled.

By the time Annie returned, the conservatory was finished. Martin had purchased new furniture, bookshelves and even had a local artist paint some pictures to compliment the look. The doors to the conservatory opened out onto the freshly mowed garden and there was chilled champagne and strawberries to officially welcome Annie back. When Martin saw Annie and her new look, he held his hand up to cover his eyes, he took a step back, then a few more, stumbled and crashed onto the glass table that held the champagne and strawberries. He lay on the floor clutching his chest while Annie rang for an ambulance. By the time they arrived he was dead, a sudden heart attack. Annie sat on the new velvet sofa in the conservatory and watched the paramedics wheel Martin's body out of the house. She checked her profile in her mirror compact and brushed her hair. She then called her hairdresser and nail technician and booked an appointment for later that afternoon. She wanted to be ready and looking her best for when she returned to work the next day.

The next morning, Annie joined the staff meeting and greeted everyone with a smile and cookies she had purchased while abroad. Dylan gave Annie a warm hug and told her she looked great. He introduced her to Susie who had been offered a position in the company. People chatted among themselves waiting for the president to show up to deliver his morning briefing. By the time he arrived, everyone had been told about the sudden death of Annie's husband, Dylan had offered to take over her work for as long as she needed, and Annie reassured everyone that she needed to keep busy. The president walked to the front of the room, facing his employees. He cast his gaze across the faces of those gathered there and then did a double-take when his eyes landed on Annie. He could not take his eyes of her. It was the second time that year that an employee at the company had fallen in love at first sight. Within a week, Annie was sharing her new conservatory with the president of her company.

Waiting in dreams

When they meet it is a rainy autumn morning. I'm not suggesting the day was very different from any other this time of year. In fact, most of the autumn days merge together in this part of the world. The rain is intermittent, heavy then light then a pause before a downpour. That's what I mean by 'rainy'. The sky is overcast without a cloud in sight. It is grey and rainy. I like to be specific about some things, but not all.

Moving on ... the cafe on the corner of Marchmont and Tyler is in a refurbished red brick. Industrial lamps hang from the high ceiling and there are an odd assortment of velvet sofas, oak chairs and wobbly tables populated by youthful looking people from the local college and weary workers from nearby offices.

It is here that Adam Watkins meets his secret crush. Okay, wait, there's more to it than that.

Adam rushes into the cafe, having caught the tail end of the downpour. He is soaked and pushes back his hair wondering if he has time to make himself look presentable and maybe even appealing. But he knows he is already late. With an audible sigh, he scans the cafe, his gaze landing on a lone man sitting on a green velvet sofa. He starts to raise his hand in a wave then lowers it quickly, thinking better of it. He doesn't want to attract any attention — any more than he already has. His anxiety kicks in, he is late, he looks a mess and he is meeting Ivan Martinez, who looks even more incredible in real life than he expected.

This is it, Adam thinks to himself. He takes in two sharp breaths and walks forward.

"I refuse a goal oriented life," says Ivan.

Of course he does, thinks Adam. He clears his throat, "Yet, here you are! A model slash actor slash musician slash activist slash psychologist! Where do you find the energy and time?"

Ivan shrugs and slumps back into the green velvet sofa. Adam wants to join him. He feels blessed, envious and aroused all rolled into one. He hadn't expected Ivan to be so likeable. Gorgeous, great personality, successful and likeable - Adam is surprised he is managing to hold a conversation. Every part of his body is tingling. "And your fans? Can they expect you to do more shows next year?"

"Well, I really want to maintain a connection with those who like my work. I want to get out there and spend more time with my admirers. But it has been difficult for me. I have had so many competing demands on my time. Also, I'm just one person, you know. I want to have time to do my own things too."

Adam nods. He won't add that to the article. No one wants the mundane. He needs something that will blow the socks of his editor, or there's no way he'll be getting another high profile assignment like this one. Ivan smiles. Adam pushes back his damp hair conscious of the smile and gaze. His mind wondering again. Did he really want this assignment to advance his career or was meeting his crush more important? In a flash after 15 years of struggling in the industry, Adam puts attraction, ahead of his ambitions. Adam who has been single for over five years and has pretty much eschewed the dating scene in preference for a life invested in his journalism and photography.

Ivan misreads the situation. He thinks he hasn't been clear or the journalist has failed to understand the things he has been talking about. Perhaps he hasn't been interesting enough.

"Okay, I'll let you in on a secret. Just between you and me, I'll be playing the Halcyon Arena next spring. There! Put that in your article!"says Ivan. "It hasn't been announced to even my manager yet."

Adam looks relieved and while Ivan interprets this as being because he has offered up a tantalising secret, in fact Adam has caught sight of his reflection in the mirror behind them and he doesn't look as bad as he thought he did. At the same time he has decided that he wants free tickets to the event and a solid date with Ivan. So he pushes for more information. He realises that in a spate of 30 minutes rather than getting over his crush, he has crash landed and fallen heavily for Ivan Martinez. How often does this happen to people on meeting Ivan face to face he wonders. Is it everyone? Ivan speaks with grace and empathy, with a real understanding of helping people and also his responsibilities as a role model. For some, this would be a turn off, there is only so much goodness that can be tolerated, but for Adam, it's an added attraction, the sincerity merely makes Ivan all the more desirable.

Ivan eyes Adam cautiously. He has only just realised that Adam came for him not for the article. He curses himself for taking so long to catch on. He makes a snap judgement against his more considered temperament. He has been around Adam's type before, he thinks. Quick to fall and needy as hell. He'd never hear the end of it if he took this one home and worse, Adam looked like someone who thought he looked good. And he did, thought Ivan, nodding to something Adam was saying while looking him over. Adam was easy on the eye, but Ivan had been bruised many times. Still, he was curious and perhaps a little bored. How harmful could it be to entertain a little late afternoon fun with a journalist who clearly revelled at getting his first shot at a major article, but had put that aside because of his crush?

Before you write Ivan off, consider this. He sought love and companionship when younger and had his heart broken in all the places it could break without rendering him closed to the possibility of loving again. Like so many who age well, have classic good looks and a healthy bank account he has many admirers but none feel genuine enough and few are able to look past his public persona to glimpse the man who secretly held on to kindness and love as the only way out of a future without creative pursuits and tenderness.

The rain has become unrelenting. Accompanied by strong winds, the windows in the apartment take a battering. Adam doesn't notice. Lying in Ivan's arms, he is worried and nervous. He confessed his strong desire for Ivan in words then in action. But now he feels different, on the tip of his tongue are the words 'never leave me'. Her cringes inside and sincerely hopes that Ivan didn't mean what he said, "let's have some fun and see how it goes." Adam ignored it, hoping it was just standard fare. Nothing was supposed to happen anyhow. Ivan had invited him over to see his collection of movie stills and artwork. They had spent the afternoon together talking and exploring their philosophies, finding common ground and contradictions in their convictions. When it came time to leave Adam blurted out "I'm really into you Ivan." He was out of breath when he spoke those words and felt both relieved and ridiculously inept. He had wanted to say something far more poetic that afternoon, but for once was lost, completely adrift from his words. Ivan, didn't blink, he merely accepted Adam's embrace and hungry kisses, revelling in an afternoon of passion, humorous interludes and long embraces.

Well, the thing is, with Adam in his arms, it slowly dawned on Ivan that he had actually fallen hard for Adam. Terrified, he feels his body stiffen. He doesn't know how this has happened and he is very unhappy because he called it fun before waiting to see how he felt.

It is a cold spring day and there is frost on the ground. It is thick so you can hear the crisp crunch under your boots. Ivan and Adam have made it to the sixth year of their relationship without major upheaval. They have hardly spent any time away from each other since that autumn afternoon. Neither has seen their career suffer, in fact both have found new audiences for their work. They are seen in public often together as an affectionate couple. They are very caring in private too.

No, there isn't any more to this tale.
This happens sometimes — a happy ending.

Last night in Copenhagen

The hotel was tucked into the corner of a busy, small street. You could have missed it if you didn't know what to look for. It used to be a clothing warehouse on five floors, when this part of the city served the textile trade. Like so many parts of the city, this area too had succumbed to the bourgeoning tourist trade, although this area was considered to be more eclectic and certainly attracted art connoisseurs all year round. The hotel retained many of the features of the original construction and attracted high end clientele who wanted something different from traditional fare.

Henry Latimer and Elle Scott were no different in that respect. Both were well to do. For them, the place offered privacy, no questions asked and they were least likely to run into anyone they knew.

The 'Hotel' neon sign flickered colouring Henry's pale grey face in shades of red, green and blue. A gust of warm air blew through the open window, the light voile curtains shifting. Sounds of sirens, and arguments could be heard in the distance. Most thought it added to the ambience of the place, to hear the heart of a busy city, but Henry has come to feel otherwise. On their last few stays he wanted to tell Elle to find somewhere else. But he always forgot to mention it or perhaps he couldn't think of anywhere else that afforded him the anonymity this place did.

He no longer finds anything about this hotel interesting or culturally awakening. He just doesn't. Time changes his perception of objects, buildings, people and his own life. He thinks it's the same for other people, but he can't be sure. Perception being what it is, how could he ever know what others perceive? His absolutist views don't get him very far. He finds it difficult to accept or hold on to core beliefs so he can communicate properly with others, make connections and all those things his therapist tells him he must do. He doesn't believe her. He goes to therapy because it gives him a chance to talk without feeling guilty that someone has to hear him — he pays her to listen after all. Maybe it is because of all the talking but he feels vacant, an absorbing emptiness has taken over him and he has embraced it like a new home.

The ceiling light dims as if there is a power surge. Henry sits quietly on the edge of the bed, blinking slowly. His back is turned away from Elle. She has memorised the placement of the freckles on his shoulders and the soft downward slope to his lean arm. Used to curling up behind him, clutching him to her and feeling his back snug against her, she resists the temptation now of reaching for him. He is the first person Elle has ever enjoyed lying next to. Henry is always just the right temperature, not too hot and never sticky, even during summer months. He has a faint scent of meadows in bloom, even though he wears no bottled scent. His scent is comforting to her.

Elle wants to hold Henry longer tonight. But the thing is beautiful Elle knows Henry wants to leave and is thinking about the best way to do it. She thinks he is wondering whether she will scream and grab him, prevent him from reaching the door. Maybe he imagines she will pick up the heavy silver bed lamp and hit him over the head with it, wanting him to die for even thinking of leaving.

Elle stretches her leg out and gives him a sharp kick. He falls off the bed with a thud. She giggles and he laughs, raising one eyebrow. In any other situation, they would be considered a well matched couple. Him with his long pauses, thoughtful glances and measured approach to everything he does. Elle complimenting him with her enthusiasm and generosity, her patience, giving him time to make his decisions.

Henry peers at Elle from the floor. His soft hair is ruffled, it needs a comb. He always forgets, just runs his hands through it, as if that will suffice. His hair has thinned since they first met, and there are flecks of white. Imperceptible to most, but Elle notices. She loves playing with his hair, twirling her fingers round the loose curls and breathing in deeply. She has gripped the ringlets at the base of his neck, pulling him to her for a kiss and holding him longer than he wants her to when he leaves for home. The first time they kissed he said it didn't feel right. So she kissed him again, and again until it did. It never felt wrong for her. She never told him that. After their first kiss, she wanted nothing except to give herself to Henry completely. All her ambitions fell away. All her past unhappinesses meant nothing. Henry was all that mattered. Henry was all Elle wanted.

If only Henry felt the same way, he never did. Henry was an explorer of life who never stayed anywhere for long or with anyone. His heart and mind were always ready for the next thing. That hadn't changed with therapy. In fact it had magnified. He was ready to move away from Elle, call a halt to their monthly rendezvous. Was she thinking of making things more permanent he wondered? Then decided he didn't care, for he couldn't offer her that.

Elle was someone who always believed in finding the one person to compliment her. When she met Henry the other aspects of her life caved into him. She spent her time thinking about their time together. Sure, yes, she wanted more. Of course she did. But six years later here she was, still waiting for him to ask her to be his. She didn't dare broach the subject herself of course. For she knew (she really did) that he would walk away and then where would she be? Alone without Henry, without her meadow and sweet, sweet kisses.

You would think Elle had grown tired of waiting by now. But she hadn't. His lack of commitment and desire to be owned by her and her by him, just made her want him more. It had inflated her desires and sustained their passionate relationship for far longer than many settled couples could have hoped. So there they were, two people, coming together once a month, both knowing they were going nowhere. Was it important for them to see what they had as a journey and a progressive one at that? Or could they just last like this until they no longer needed the embrace of each other?

Henry sat back against the headboard and circled his arm around Elle, pulling her to him. She rested on his chest and felt his warmth. It was always like this towards the end of their time together. She would tell herself she could no longer take the tension of seeing him leave and waiting and waiting until she saw him again. But she would tell herself that if she only waited a little longer he would ask her what she wanted to hear. Will you be with me Elle? Will you be mine?

She would always tell herself that he would say that. It was just a matter of time. So what if he was taking longer than most? She wanted him and that was all that mattered. Then she would get anxious wondering what she would do if he failed to show the following month. What would she do then? She would have missed her opportunity to ask him about building something, anything together. She wanted to be bound to him, more than in spirit, more than in her constant thoughts of him, his words, his scent, his presence.

Henry turned to Elle and kissed her gently on her lips, like he always did before rising from the bed to pack his things. At this point Elle would always loose her composure and shed a tear. She would wipe it away quickly of course, but Henry would always turn round at precisely that moment and notice. He would shrug and turn back and then as if to change his mind, he would leave his bag for a while and come over to her and give her a little hug. Tell her they would meet again. Then nudge her on the shoulder like an old friend and say, "Cheer up."

Elle pictured herself reaching for the lamp and hitting Henry over the head in one swift move. There would be no way he would leave then. Her fists were balled up, like the last time and her nails dug into her palms. She let out a deep sigh. Could she hang on for another month? Could she wait to talk to him face to face or should she just send him a text when he left, tell him it's over and that she could take no more. She got up and went to the bathroom, looked at herself in the mirror and drank some water. Henry came in like he always did, kissed her on the shoulder and said, "Goodbye Elle."

Technical
misunderstandings

Charlie Oden waits his turn seemingly patient, but on the inside he is in turmoil. There's just one more customer ahead of him and they're taking their time deciding on a colour for a phone case. Charlie shifts from foot to foot, repositioning the bag under his arm. The customer finally opts for a purple case. They take their time thanking Linda, the shop owner, for her patience and time. She nods solemnly, so the customer thanks her once more, and again, until Linda thanks them for their custom. Satisfied, the customer leaves. No sooner does the door close than Charlie places his bag on the counter, and as if he has run several miles, huffs and puffs through his tale of woe.

"My speaker has been taken over by China! I put my music on play this morning and the speaker refused to connect. Yes, I was using bluetooth, but I also have a USB cable to charge it, which I keep connected all the time, so it never runs out. So, I took out the cable and switched it on and it announced, 'Bluetooth connected'. So then I hit play on the song on my notepad. It began playing. Then I plugged the USB cable into the back of my speaker and it said something in a Chinese language and stopped working." Charlie breathes heavily. Linda frowns and brings him a chair, so he can sit at the counter. Charlie has one of those faces that is smooshed inwards and his lips are permanently sagged downwards. A bit like the face of a bulldog after it has run out of treats.

Linda crosses her arms. She rocks back and forth on her trainers, "Chinese eh? Which Chinese language?"

"I don't know!" says Charlie, sitting back in the chair.

"You didn't check? You didn't ask Siri?"

"No, what difference would it make?"

"You never know. How can you be certain it is a Chinese language?"

Charlie scratches his forehead. "Siri? How will it fix my speaker? It has been taken over by China."

"The Chinese have no intention of taking over mid-market speakers."

"How do you know that?"

"Hey, did you wake up this morning and decide to make my life difficult?" asks Linda.

"No. I just want my speaker to work so I can listen to music, like I do every morning. Can you help or not?"

Linda brings her laptop over and sits next to Charlie. She types "why is my bluetooth speaker speaking Chinese?" into the search bar. She looks over at Charlie and offers him a tea.

Charlie nods solemnly, "I'm lucky you are round the corner really. Otherwise what would I do?"

Linda reaches for the speaker and plugs it in.

"Here, be careful with that. It does the job and I want it to keep doing that."

"Of course Charlie. I'll make sure this second hand five pound speaker works until they lay you to rest in one of the Co-op coffins."

"The cheek of it!"

Linda smiles watching Charlie drain his cup of tea. She must remember to buy some biscuits for next week.

"While you're at it, can you check for listening devices? I don't need any of that spyware on it," says Charlie.

Linda rolls her eyes. "Shall I check for hidden cameras and miniature spy robots as well?"

"Oi, enough of that cheek! I paid you good money for the speaker, I expect it to last, like everything I bought from Woolworths."

"Woolworths? Well that brings back no memories for me!" Linda laughs wiping down the speaker and putting it back in Charlie's bag.

"Woolworths … Now there was a shop. None of this scan your own items rubbish. There were always two people at checkout, spoke to you nice and even packed the bag for you."

"Wonderful! What do you think I've been doing all these years for you Charlie?"

Charlie waves his hand in the air and kisses his teeth.

"Bluetooth disconnected," says the voice from the speaker, followed by "Bluetooth connected."

"Sounds very English to me," says Linda, switching the speaker on and off a number of times to check.

Charlie huffs and rises, straightening his trousers. He is tired but glad his speaker is fixed. Of course he is not going to offer Linda a penny for her troubles. Why should he? Didn't he buy the damn thing from her shop?

Charlie takes the bag from the counter and thanks her reluctantly. He looks at her a little longer than needed, then shakes his head as if to bring himself back to the present.

Linda nods and crosses her arms. She walks behind him, waves and shuts the door behind him. Another week, another goodbye. It has been this way for over a year. This is the only interaction Linda has with Charlie, her father, these days. He comes to her electrical store once a week with a different question, sometimes just to browse. He doesn't recognise her as his daughter anymore, but some part of his brain impels him to visit her. Linda closes the store for the day and walks home to her empty flat, hoping one day her father will recognise her, his memory coming back to what it once was.

Glorious land

It is still a concern these days. Perhaps if we had dealt with it better when it first started. But it still happens, the loud sounds of car horns being beeped as they screech past, the knocking on our doors in the middle of the night, the giggling and the rubbish strewn in our small gardens.

I mean just a month ago, Jameson Knight was startled by fire crackers going off in his front porch at one in the morning. He was so shocked he tumbled out of bed and fell on his cat. And that was not the worst of it. Jess Williams was walking her dog Edmund after Sunday lunch last week and was hit in the face by a ham sandwich which was pitched right at her out of a passing van.

You see, Brier Tree Lane was the site of a clash between the people who lived there and motorists who used it as a short cut to the main road. This happened a way back, at least 5 years ago now. The residents had taken the issue up with the police, the local councillors and even their Member of Parliament. There were already speed bumps on the road and relevant signage. So, the councillors felt that they had done all they could to deter reckless drivers. The police patrolled the area at peak times and believed that they had discharged their duties.

The Member of Parliament was more difficult to pin down. She was against limiting access to Brier Tree Lane, especially given her commitment to increasing tourism in the village and surrounding area. The other reason was less obvious to begin with, it was only revealed much later in the dispute, that the minister herself had been caught speeding numerous times, and was drunk in charge of a vehicle on one occasion.

After over two years of letter writing campaigns and petitions, the residents decided to escalate their actions with hope and courage. None of them wanted to sell up and move, heavens few could afford to do so. And who would buy their homes? When Jeffrey Smithers put his on the market, he received one paltry offer of half what he had paid for because of the noise pollution from the traffic and the danger it posed on such a small lane. Imagine! Half the price he paid! The poor man would not be able to buy another retirement home after a lifetime of saving. After all the publicity about the noise and traffic, no one wanted to move to Brier Tree Lane. So the residents were stuck, and the traffic just became more unrelenting. It was Jameson and Jess who came up with the plan to strike back. They could take no more, so they decided to try and slow the traffic down by putting their own signs up on the road. One sign read 'This is a quiet residential area, please use alternative routes'. Another read, 'Please drive through slowly, residents walk here'. After a day, both signs were knocked over. So they put up two new signs, with harsher language 'Don't you dare drive fast! Show some respect!'. Jameson felt the exclamation points would really show everyone they were serious. Jess, was less enthused and argued strongly that the 'F-word' should be used, albeit in moderation. I think you get the idea.

After many attempts, the residents gave up on signage and put barricades along the lane instead. A couple of bales of hay, a few traffic cones — that kind of thing. And this is when things began to change. The motorists began using the lane as a race course, dodging the barriers and doing sharp turns. It just made things worse and attracted a whole new calibre of driver. But the residents were committed to defending their patch. Soon large rocks were placed along the lane, sometimes hidden under leaves. Next a huge pile of logs was dropped at the entrance to the lane. Of course the police became involved. "You can't just barricade a road," they said exasperated. But the residents didn't stop. If the barricades were removed, then more appeared the next day. The police were reluctant to make any arrests at first, but then were left with little choice. At one point, all seven residents were arrested. The story made the national press and Brier Tree Lane became even busier with the arrival of photographers and journalists and those who took the side of the residents and wanted to show their support, and those who were angry at what was considered to be the flagrant disrespect shown to motorists and their right to use the lane.

But it wasn't until Jeffrey Smithers got into an altercation with one of the photographers that things actually spiralled out of control. Car tires were slashed, one resident used chestnuts and a catapult to damage windscreens, another decided to lie in the middle of the road and people from other parts of the country came along to show their support for non-violent protest. It was quite a year. Finally, the councillors gave in. They decided to shut the lane to general traffic, reduce the size of the lane, and block off the entrance which fed into the main road. The residents were finally able to sleep soundly at night and walk their dogs safely during the day. And for a while it was fine. It really was.

But then the racers appeared, unconcerned there was a dead end, they just raced up and down the road. It tickled them to annoy the elderly residents. At least that is what Jess said it was. But Jameson thought otherwise, and that was why his property was targeted more than others. Jameson took it on himself to record the racers, track them down and pay their parents and employers a visit. The embarrassment caused a great deal of anger among the racers, plus their parents threatened to bar them from driving their cars. This caused great consternation. The racers had little else to do in the village but focus on their cars. So, one of them decided to stand as a local councillor and won. Before long Brier Tree Lane was opened up to motorists again and would stay that way for five years, with the residents suffering through daily agitation by motorists who had read the story on social media and were overwhelmingly taking the side of the right to drive lobby.

The police gave up, mainly because their budget was slashed and there were lots of other antisocial behaviour in the village to keep them occupied.

So, back to the night that Jameson heard firecrackers and landed on his cat Matthew. He spent the next week travelling to and from the nearest town as Matthew was admitted to the veterinary surgery for a broken leg. Jameson was angry, and it turned into fury when he took Matthew home with a splint and saw the vet bill. He hit the roof and took out his shotgun. Later when Jess got hit in the face with a ham sandwich while walking her dog Edmund, she too decided to take up arms — her choice was a long pitchfork. Edmund ran round in circles while she stood in the middle of the road, her eyes ablaze, thrusting the pitch fork forward and bringing traffic to a halt. Meanwhile, Jameson stood on his balcony and fired off a round of shots. Bang, bang and another bang.

Edmund grew even more agitated at the sound of gunshots. One of the motorists got out of their car and tussled with Jess for the pitchfork and she tripped, falling to the ground. Edmund growled and bit the motorist hard on the calf. He stumbled in pain and fell forward, landing on the pitchfork.

The incident meant that Brier Tree Lane was shut permanently and an investigation ensued.

Jameson at the age of 84 was questioned about the firearms and Jess was taken in for observation due to the fall. Jameson was released and Jess came home from hospital after a couple of days with a minor concussion. Edmund remained at her side.

When the accidental death of the motorist was announced in the press it enraged the racers and other motorists further. They approached a local developer and campaigned for the destruction of the houses on Brier Tree Lane and the expansion of the lane to feed into the main road.

And so, in the fifth year, the fight continues. Jameson sits watching the road most days with his rifle in hand and Jess and Edmund trek up and down the road, diverting motorists. Some residents have spent a fortune trying to sound proof their homes and others have given up, taking a loss on their property, selling it to developers, and moving on to quieter, safer spots. Most of the councillors lost their seats in election and so did the Member of Parliament. Many blamed it on the saga of Brier Tree Lane.

Puffles goes into a sulk

It didn't seem to matter what Aria Atkinson did. Elliott Masters wasn't responding. This morning, in her frustration, she threw the sofa cushions across the room in a rage. She also lost her temper, quite unnecessarily, with Puffles, her two year old dog. Puffles still hadn't forgiven Aria for last week when she forgot to feed her after getting drunk, throwing plates on the floor and falling asleep in the hallway all because Elliott didn't call.

Puffles kept her distance from Aria all week, hiding away under the stairs next to her food bowl. This morning she refused to sit on Aria's lap during work calls. She positioned herself on the windowsill over looking the city, glancing over at Aria to see if she noticed. Aria hadn't. She was too absorbed in thinking about Elliott and fielding work calls at the same time. Puffles gave her one last look and then resigned herself to another day on her own. She sighs and slumps on the window sill, lost without the attention she used to receive and the company Aria used to provide her with. She no longer feels safe.

Aria slumped back heavily against her swivel chair. She ruffled her hair and rubbed her face, willing herself not to loose hope. Even with the ten texts she sent this morning, the two letters she posted last week, the hourly emails and calls to his office and home, Elliott was not responding to her. So, nothing had changed. She had kept up this level of communication for over a week. She did not for a moment think she was overdoing it. While in the past if a boyfriend ghosted her she would merely switch off her phone, buy herself a treat, sleep off the rejection and just get on with it, it was different with Elliott. She was not letting him go that easily. She couldn't. He had gotten to her in ways she hadn't realised someone could. He caused emotions to rise in her, some of which she couldn't even name. Her skin tingled just from saying his name.

She put her headset on. The meeting began. She turned the sound on, greeted the others and waited. The director began his presentation and now there was no risk of Aria or any of the team being called on to say anything. Aria switched her camera off, and drank her camomile tea. She opened her journal and added to the list of things she needed to do to try and capture Elliott's attention. She read some of her entries and admonished herself for not trying harder.

Aria wasn't someone who gave up easily anyway. In fact, she was a firm believer that most people didn't know what was good for them, and that people like her just needed to show them and convince them what was best.

She and Elliott were meant to be together and that was that. They had so much in common, plus there was a whole lifetime for them to explore together and she knew she could make him happier than he imagined or anyone else could.

She slapped her thighs, rousing herself to think of what to do next. Her persistence had never failed her before, why should it now?

She decided to search for a perfect gift for Elliott. He always loved presents, he would definitely speak to her then, she thought. She just needed to find the right one. How hard could that be? She had researched everything she could about him. After an hour, she settled on a striking dark blue velvet blazer from Elliott's favourite designer. It was pricey but would go perfectly with the shirt and tie she got him for his birthday, she thought. She smiled happily, imagining how it would look on him. The blazer would go so well with his looks. She held back a tear. Hoping she would be there to see it. He would realise how much she cared wouldn't he? There was so much thought that had gone into the gift. He would realise this.

Aria closed her eyes, willing Elliott to appear before her. Tomorrow morning he would return from his jog, have a shower and have a coffee and muffin. His routine. The door bell would ring. He would be surprised and touched by the gift, and regret being silent for so long. He would come over to hers straight away and apologise. He would take her out for brunch and he would cancel all his appointments choosing to spend the day with her instead.

Aria opened her eyes and clicked the online shopping cart and entered Elliott's details. She added the special gift wrap with the message, 'For you Elliott, Love Aria'.

Elliott and Aria had been together for three months. That was a long time for both of them. She was fully invested in the relationship. She considered herself lucky to be part of his life. Elliott was this debonair, well-connected artist, with admirers across the globe and he had picked Aria to be his one and only. Well, at least that was Aria's interpretation. According to her it had started out as a steamy embrace after late night drinks at his sold out art show. She was surprised and flattered when she felt his eyes linger on her. When they finally kissed, Aria swore off seeing anyone else. It is unclear at this point if Elliott thought the same, but never mind.

Aria was an art student, in the fifth year of trying to complete her PhD. She had spent the summer working at the upmarket gallery where Elliott had a show. She was hired for her looks — the gallery owner said so. It didn't bother her. But Aria could barely believe Elliott considered her attractive, and worthy of his attention. He moved in exclusive circles. The last two people he had been photographed with were up and coming models — runway models! And he had chosen her that night!

Aria began to ignore her loyal companion Puffles at about this point — in other words the day she met Elliott. She spent all her time thinking about Elliott, waiting for his call, sending him messages, buying him gifts and meeting him when he was free. She regularly forgot to take Puffles on walks and rarely spoke to her like she used to. She sometimes forgot Puffles shared her apartment and she also ignored most of her friends. Aria was swept up in Elliott, his opinions about art, politics, fashion and so much more. She hung on his every word and after the first month dedicated her time to finding out more about him and reading up on subjects he was interested in. She never imagined being with anyone else once they got together.

After the summer Aria took a well paid job at an advertising firm and moved closer to Elliott, just round the corner in fact. It meant she could work from home, work on her PhD and be ready to meet Elliott whenever he was available at short notice. He didn't need to travel across town either. Elliott had a busy schedule. But Aria was always grateful that he had time for her, even if it had begun to seem that their time together was becoming shorter and shorter.

Puffles was happy at first when Aria stayed home, thinking that would be the last of Elliott.

However, she was unhappy at the move, she was further away from the park and her friends. She could no longer watch the squirrels go about their day either. Also it soon became obvious that it was because of Elliott that Aria was at home and that she would just feel the pain of being ignored that much more. With Aria spending her money on her new boyfriend, Puffles got fewer and fewer treats and her stash of chew toys grew smaller and smaller. But worst of all, Elliott insisted that Puffles get locked in the laundry room when he stayed over. And Aria didn't even protest. Puffles had been her best friend and confidant and now this. The laundry room was cold and the floor chilly. It was a very difficult situation and the terrier was feeling terribly alone. So, when she saw Aria order Elliott yet another gift that morning, she decided to take matters into her own paws. She would play second fiddle no more, certainly not to Elliott who merely made nonsensical marks on canvas. Certainly Puffles felt she outshone Elliott in all areas.

The next morning, Puffles slipped out of the apartment and made her way to Elliotts house. She got there just in time for the post, sneaking through the front door when Elliott opened it to get his mail. He almost didn't see her, but her tail accidentally brushed up against his ankle and he shrieked. It startled her so she barked and ran round the living room and up the stairs knocking things over. She could hear him yelling and later speak harshly on the phone to Aria.

When Puffles finally stopped running through the house, she peered down from the top of the stairs to see Elliott wearing his new blazer and studying himself in the hallway mirror. She could feel the rise of anger. How could he accept the gift after ignoring Aria? Also, would all these gifts soon mean she would have no food? What was going to happen to her? Was Elliott ever going to just leave? Puffles wanted her friend back and the more she thought about it, the greater her anguish, fear and temper.

With two swift leaps Puffles pounced on Elliott, teeth sinking into the side of his neck. Elliott howled and fell to the ground clutching his neck in horror. Puffles sat on top of him and set about ripping the beautiful blue blazer to shreds. Elliott tried to push her off but failed, such was her intense concentration. Puffles was lost in her pent up anger and had unleashed all of it.

It was quite a sight when Aria arrived. Elliott had told her to come and pick up her wretched dog when he first saw Puffles in his home, he hadn't even thanked her for the blazer or asked her how she was. When Aria stepped into the hall, she saw Elliott half conscious on the floor and Puffles sitting on top of him, still growling, the blazer in tatters. Elliott asked for help. But Aria refused until he proposed to her, or at least said they would be engaged. She begged and pleaded with him while calling emergency services and also finding the time to reprimand Puffles.

It was at this point that Elliott told her to get lost and take Puffles with her. He never wanted to see either of them again. He was tired of being pestered by her although he did like the blue blazer — but look what her badly behaved dog had done. He then fainted from the loss of blood. As for Aria, she started to wail, pushing and prodding Elliott to try to get him to wake up. She thought he was going to die, and it would be her fault. She kissed him tenderly and begged for forgiveness for pushing him. She was beside herself.

When Puffles realised that Aria had come for Elliott and not her, she became so upset she trembled and whined. Aria told her to keep quiet. That was all Puffles could take, she pounced on Aria and nipped her ankle. Aria fell back. She lay twitching next to Elliott.

When the paramedics and later the police arrived they found no sign of Puffles. Both Elliott and Aria survived the attack and never spoke of it.

Their break up caught no one in their inner circle (or outer for that matter) by surprise. In fact most hadn't expected it to last so long. Some hadn't even realised they were dating. Aria never got over the end of the relationship. When she got home Puffles was sitting on the sofa. Aria decided to give Puffles away to her mum. And so Puffles was banished from the city and sent to live in the countryside. She was upset at first, but once she saw the squirrels and the green fields, she was much happier and went on to live a long and contented life.

As for Aria, she funnelled all her heartbreak into her art and eventually became a prolific and popular artist in her own right. But nothing could quell the loss of Elliott not even the revelation that at no point was he faithful to her.

As for Elliott, he fell out of favour, no one really knows why, but after the incident with Puffles, he was unable to focus on his work. He was fine though, his previous work had set him up with a healthy retirement fund and he continued to be in demand at art events.

In the end there is me

I sit silently in front of the large blue screen, clicking the mouse when a red box appears. I drag the red box into a folder on the desktop. I imagine Geetha is at the other end of the building, watching her screen for the red box too. I wonder who the others are, whether there are more of us. I can't tell and I haven't been told.

I met Geetha by chance. We take the same bus to this place. She told me we weren't supposed to speak to each other after she sat next to me, introduced herself and offered me a hot breakfast roll. I shrugged at the time, munching on the roll. It was soft and buttery. Gheeta makes them herself. That's what she wants to do. Run a bakery in her neighbourhood. She says they need one. All the other shops sell food that is bad for you and even unbranded alcohol. I nod while enjoying the roll. I hoped we would meet again like this, but after two weeks, gave up. I wish I had taken her number or email.

My back doesn't hurt so much today. Margot gave me a massage when I got home and she sewed a back support garment you can wear after finding the pattern online. It goes well with my binder, which is another reason for my back pain. Margot knows I need this job, just like she needs hers. We want to move once we save enough, but it is difficult with the wage freeze. We have been trying to leave the city for four years, maybe this year we will make it. Margot works from home. She checks documents and deletes them on systems. At least that's what she tells me. I don't really understand it or care. She got the job last December. It makes a real difference let me tell you, now she doesn't have to pay to travel to work like me.

I look back at my screen. I have another five hours left on the night shift. Yeah, that's the other problem with this job, there are a lot of night shifts. And it isn't planned. I just get a text to tell me to do a shift. Come to think about it, maybe Geetha isn't here. She may not be on night shift duty tonight.

I stretch my arms upwards. The heating is switched off at 5pm. So this bunker gets cold. I bought a small fan heater and plug it in when it gets really chilly. The bunker used to store old passenger aeroplanes until the bottom fell out of the illegal travel industry. Yeah, people didn't want to risk it after governments finally admitted that they knew about illegal travel all along. So, the man who set up this company, bought these bunkers and put us in them. There are ten bunkers in all. Each of us have a bunker to ourselves. There is a small fridge and a coffee machine next to my desk and a toilet at the entrance. To get in I swipe my card and my prints are scanned. If I feel unwell or need something I push the red buzzer under my table and a support worker appears. Not a real person obviously. It is a virtual projection and I speak to them. I've seen the guards at the entrance, but they are hard to speak to. They are robots, highly skilled and efficient. You can speak to them on subjects like the weather. But, in general, we are not supposed to engage with them. Geetha told me someone she knew lost their life trying to tease one of the robot guards by asking it to do back flips. It shot him.

My screen is filing up with red boxes so I click on them rapidly. I don't know what my work is about. This is how it is. I filled out a form, was interviewed online, and then given the job. I didn't meet another human being in the process. It is all managed by algorithms and robots. You do get feedback though. I was told there were 10,200 applicants for this job. I was grateful to get it. Let me tell you. Apart from clicking on the red boxes when they appear and storing them in the desktop folder, I also have to fill in a report if I see boxes of any other colour appear on screen. It happens occasionally. I am supposed to ignore them and fill in a report and send it by email to a generic mail box. I am not allowed to listen to music or take calls or use headphones. Apart from that, there are no other stipulations. I don't know who my manager is, but I have had two reports on job performance since starting here three years ago. Both positive and the last one gave me a promotion. I am now called 'controller' previously I was named 'clearer'.

I think back to my conversation with Geetha two weeks ago. Imagine working somewhere and only meeting a colleague three years into the job. That's how it is in most places these days. You're lucky if you have a team, and you see them regularly. Most people have solitary jobs. Even in schools and hospitals. Robots do everything and cost less. In medicine, they are faster at making a diagnosis and more accurate. Outcomes have improved although most people can't afford healthcare. In schools, robots educate children at a faster rate and for specific jobs they are identified for. I'm much older and can remember a time when people were everywhere and you couldn't get through a day without talking to someone face to face.

It's not like we didn't expect this. Many felt it happened too quickly though. I don't know. I don't want to make a judgement about it. I'm too scared. I hear things on the bus, that people disappear if they speak out loud about their jobs. None of us are supposed to say anything once we leave our place of work. We mustn't discuss our jobs with others either or share anything about what we do. It doesn't matter that most of us don't even know what we do anymore, we just do as we are told to get paid and to have enough to eat and somewhere to live.

I can remember a time when we had something called a career and we could talk about it as much as we wanted. In fact it was the first thing anyone asked you 'What do you do for a living?'. These days we just talk about the weather.

I'm lucky I have Margot in my life. Without her, I would be as lost. Margot is my partner and has been since I graduated. She and I have stuck together through all the changes. We are one of the few in the city to be in a relationship.

For a while, it was thought that people would find partners easily through work and dating apps. But that all fell away when visual projections and robots took off. Now everyone lives with both, they don't need another human, or want one. That's what Margot tells me anyway. She seems to get the news from somewhere about things like that. I don't.

Most of the city is empty so we don't see people regularly. Even when we do, on buses or trains, no one says very much and we are told to avoid eye contact if we can.

We don't know who we are communicating with anymore - could be robots of some sort or other organic-based human replicas. If you read the news or anything else you have to decide on a filter, pick one that suits you. There is so much information out there all from different sources, some just from archives. What filter you use is up to you. That's all there is. Filters. If you are against expansion then you use the orange filter. If you are pro military you use the blue filter (I think). I can't be sure. Margot uses the pink filter when she accesses the news. I tell her it's pointless because where is the truth in all this? She laughs at me. To her there is just different perspectives. That's what filters help with so you don't have to do it yourself.

Today I tell her about Geetha when I get home. I want to meet her again and I want her suggestion of how to do that. Margot rolls her eyes and ignores me while cooking supper. I offer to help but she pushes me away. "Used to be a time I was all you needed. Who is this Geetha to you?"

I am startled by her extreme response. I explain she is someone I met briefly and that I work with her. Margot refuses to be consoled. She finds it unacceptable that I want to get to know someone at work, even though the loneliness in the bunker has begun to get to me. She smashes the pan against the wall and damages her hand. "Why can't I just call her during the day?" she asks. She walks to the living room and collapses on the couch. She tells me that there is no space for Geetha. I don't know what she means.

The next day when I return from work Margot is gone and Geetha is at the stove cooking dinner. She welcomes me with a smile and we eat dinner together. I realise what has happened but I can't process the meaning of it. With Margot gone I don't want to stay either. Geetha tells me I can leave, but I can't come back. She doesn't tell me where to find Margot and when I get angry, she tells me to sit down. She is annoyed that I have changed my mind. She tells me I can't keep asking for different iterations. I don't know what she means. I insist that I see Margot again.

A little later Margot appears, but she looks different, her eyes are sunken and she looks ill. Her arms don't move like they used to.

I turn away. I don't bother asking what happened. I'm too worried about losing my job.

Susan's art

Was it Abigail Martin who made that comment? Susan Carrick could not be sure, but it annoyed and upset her. It had been 24 hours since Abigail had told the women at the party that Susan had married not twice but four times. Susan had shared that with Abigail in confidence, or at least she thought that was the understanding. But for her friend to have revealed that to everyone!

Susan's faced reddened just thinking back to it. There was a long pause, silence and some giggles. She had left soon after, unable to take the pitying looks that masked the obvious glee.

This was a circle of women who prided themselves in staying married to the same person, they saw this as success, a key achievement in their lives. That's why she told them she was on her second marriage, she didn't want them to know the truth. In fact, she had gone as far as to tell them that her husband, Bruce, from her first marriage had died suddenly from a heart attack. She didn't tell them that he had dumped her for his gym instructor. She sighed. At least she hadn't told Abigail that. And where was Bruce now? Partying on his yacht in Monaco no doubt. She was angry still. And the pain in her chest rose again. He was her first love. They met at college and were married after graduation. She had given up her aspirations to be a lawyer and supported him through graduate school instead, also helping him set up his business. Yes, it was a time worn story. Once he was established and successful, he had left her for someone half her age.

Next there was Brian. She met him as she was exiting the lawyers office on the day she signed the divorce papers. She had dropped her purse, he had picked it up and shown her to her car. He was half her age and she had wanted a fling. Her confidence had taken a battering. Could being with Brian restore that? It did, especially when he proposed four months later. Little did she know he did this for a living. Prey on vulnerable older women, marry them and profit any way he could. And he had. When she divorced him, she had to pay him a settlement. She had discovered his deceit because she had thrown him a surprise party only to find that he had a surprise of his own, lying naked in their marital bed with three college cheerleaders. And not only that, he had been buying them presents with her credit cards.

Next there was Benedict. She had enrolled in classes to pick up her studies where she left off. Benedict was the professor teaching the class. He was elegant, masterful and had an air of innocence about him. She developed a crush on him and during the summer holidays volunteered to assist with his research. It was a huge project, and she had to spend many long days doing the requisite fieldwork. But she didn't mind. Here she believed was a man who cared about his work and being just and fair. Of course when autumn came round, she could take it no longer. She made several passes at Benedict - he politely declined. She was broken hearted. But then one day, he finally said yes to a coffee. And by the following year they were married and living in his loft apartment in the city. She would work from home doing the research and attend classes when necessary. A year later she discovered that Benedict had used her work as his. She confronted him about it, and later regretted it. He reassured her that he was going to give her the recognition she deserved. He told her he understood her suspicions of men given her history, but she must learn to trust him. And so she gradually came to trust Benedict in every way she could. It became an addiction to please him. She did everything she could to make him happy.

Then at an annual lecture, she was sitting in the front row, looking up at her husband Benedict, delivering the speech, when there was a loud scream from the back of the auditorium. It turned out that Benedict had omitted to tell her that he had been married previously when teaching abroad in Japan, and in fact, was still married. His wife had tracked him down after a year and brought his child too. Susan had a breakdown when she found out. She spent six months in hospital being helped back to health.

She moved out of the apartment and the city. She never spoke to or saw Benedict.

So those were her three 'Bs' - Bruce, Brian and Benedict. She wowed to be more careful when choosing who to date — she would definitely steer clear of those with names beginning with 'B'.

Susan then spent two years in Santa Fe, living in a deserted house, painting and reading. She had given up all hope of becoming a fully qualified lawyer. It was then that she discovered her love of painting nature. She was also shocked when a local artist introduced her to a gallery owner. Within six months her artwork began to sell. It was fulfilling and she finally felt she was doing something for herself.

The gallery owner was called Bertrand, so at first Susan was weary of him and only dealt with his assistant. But once her paintings began to sell there were interviews to give and Bertrand often accompanied her on these. He was a softly spoken man with a polished demeanour that somehow managed to keep people at ease. He was also well versed in the classics and had a thorough knowledge of art across the globe. He had taken a personal interest in Susan's work because of she was untrained and yet managed to use the acrylic and oil mediums with a skill usually reserved for experts. He also liked the fact that unlike the other artists on his books she showed absolutely no interest in him. This sparked excitement in Bertrand who was used to being pursued.

Susan for her part had crossed off all men whose names began with 'B' from her prospective lovers list. She had gone on a few dates with a fellow artist who lived nearby but lost interest when he proposed. It was too soon and too sudden. Plus, Susan had no need for another marriage, or at least she thought. When she started giving interviews to local, and later the national press, she became conscious of her status as a single straight woman. It troubled her, especially since most interviews ended with her being asked whether she had a special someone. To which she had taken to winking, tapping her nose and saying it was a secret. Of course it was a lie. The question really was why she was so perturbed by it. Why not just say she preferred her own company for now? Susan decided to explore her feelings of inadequacy at being single in her artwork. And it was these pieces that drew the interest of Abigail Martin's group of society women. Between them they bought four of Susan's pieces and they were not inexpensive. They gave interviews in lifestyle magazines and displayed their purchases, causing a sharp spike in demand for Susan's pieces and pushing sales of other artists on Bertrand's books through the ceiling. Everyone benefitted from Susan's search for her underlying truth. The only person who was still perplexed, albeit with more in the bank account, was Susan herself. It didn't matter how many exploratory pieces she painted, she felt she needed a partner to complement her. She was beginning to feel more and more exposed in public, she needed someone to accompany her to events, especially since most of the time she would be the lone woman in attendance.

So when Bertrand started flirting with her, Susan capitulated against her better judgement. And within three months they were married. The ceremony was extravagant and well attended and it was there that Abigail Martin invited Susan into her inner circle of society women — none of whom worked, but all had healthy bank balances from inheritances and their husbands and were known to be among the most prolific collectors of contemporary art, especially by women.

When she first joined Abigail and her friends at events, dinners and shows, everyone was welcoming, especially with the debonair Bertrand on her arm, but at the end of most evenings it was Abigail who she would talk to, confiding in her, talking to her about the many things that made her feel less than she could be. Her life seemed to be unravelling even though her career was on the up and she was happily married to a man who clearly loved her. Abigail provided a listening ear and made all the right sympathetic noises. Susan was taken in and failed to foresee the danger. She hadn't changed much since her teenage years. Susan remained naive and trusting, even after her failed relationships and many other disappointments. And there is nothing wrong with that. It is the best way to forge alliances and make connections with people. Unfortunately, it can also put you at risk of exploitation and worse, jealous gossip. And so it was that Abigail, ahead of the latest event, shared everything about Susan with her close group of friends. In fact their response at the party had been pre-planned. They already knew about Susan's marriages. They just wanted to surprise her and humiliate her to the maximum. It is unclear if there was a purpose to their hurtful behaviour. It is hard to tell, but in general, Susan failed to see it as something to do with their own unhappiness and firmly saw it as a deficit on her part.

When she got home she slunk off to the shower and took a while to get herself together. Bertrand waited for his wife, worried because she was quiet on the ride back, but he was a firm believer in giving his wife the space she needed to think and develop. Bertrand was always a supporter of artists first, a nurturer of their talent, and he knew that there was much more that Susan had to offer.

Susan eventually emerged and spoke to Bertrand about her plans for a new show. He gave her a hug, putting her sniffling and reddened eyes to the emotional ups and downs of artists.

The next morning Susan was up early and by the evening had finished three canvases. She refused to show any of them to Bertrand and continued to work through the summer months. Painting through the day and sometimes through the night, rarely emerging from the studio for more than a plate of snacks and to refresh her drink. Bertrand left her to it, although he worried of her isolation. He went so far as to invite Abigail and some of the others over to speak to Susan, perhaps take her out, but they declined, and he never spoke to Susan about it.

At about that time a new artist arrived on the scene. David Vinton attracted a lot of attention because of his classic pieces and also his striking looks. He was snapped up by Bertrand who kept himself distracted by promoting David's work. It left him little time to worry about Susan who continued to keep herself isolated. One Sunday Bertrand invited David to their home and asked Susan to join them. She declined, but checked David's online profile. She was intrigued by his work and his origin. David apparently had no past and had simply burst onto the scene with fifteen paintings called 'When you next see me'. He refused to sell any of them, asking Bertrand to keep them on show until the prices went high enough due to the build up of interest. And his strategy worked. There was a long list of people interested in the work of the youthful and handsome David Vinton. Looks mattered in so many aspects of marketing and David ticked the most boxes.

David for his part was more interested in Susan. It was for this reason he had arrived in the city and tempted Bertrand with his work. David had seen Susan's pieces and had become a fan. It was because of her he started painting. He believed he could make a go of it and it would lead to her. Love from afar was not something David ever believed in. He thought most love was folly, superstition at best. He had no time for it. Then he saw Susan's art in a magazine and the artist herself standing next to one of the pieces. He tore the picture out, put it in his wallet and made a promise to himself that he would meet her. He didn't know what had moved him or why, he just needed to be with her. It astounded his long time friends when he made his declaration, but who were they to stop him. A couple of them even followed him to the city.

It was Abigail who made the highest offer for David's pieces. He had decided that a single buyer was needed for all fifteen in the series. He could not sell them on their own. This was a major frustration for Bertrand but because he was benefitting in other ways from the publicity he let it go. David said he would think about Abigail's offer — he wanted more, there was no doubt about it. When on his own he spent a lot of time laughing for he never saw himself as a painter and he was amused at his luck. But he still hadn't managed to meet Susan, the person he had come to see. Luck was on David's side again, for Susan had decided that she needed to speak to him. So when she put the finishing touches on her pieces in the autumn, she asked Bertrand to invite David to dinner.

Susan and David hit it off straight away. Both were novices who had struck a chord and attracted a following. David on meeting Susan fell

in love, for the first time, and the last. He didn't
understand it and neither did he want to. He
didn't even care if she knew or he ever got
together with her. He was just happy knowing he
loved her. At the same time he wanted to help
her. He sensed her unhappiness and it was also
clear from her manner of speech. She recounted
the event that had led to her self-imposed
isolation and David agreed to help her. Susan
showed him her pieces. To her, they were ugly
observances of the human condition, to David
they were full of beauty and humour. He felt that
her new work would be highly valued, more so
than her previous paintings. But that didn't seem
to be what Susan wanted. She was upset that he
considered her work pleasing. She wanted them
to reveal the shame she experienced the night of
Abigail's party. David knew her distress was real
and promised to help her any way he could. David
was the first person that Susan had spoken to
about the event. And once she heard what she had
to say out loud, she no longer felt ashamed. She
didn't feel she needed to hide away anymore. All
she had done was go on a journey to find love,
why had she taken Abigail's behaviour to heart.
She had no need for her friendship, she would
find others. It took Susan a while to recognise
how much art had given her and just what the
value of it was to her.

These days Susan paints murals on the exterior
of buildings in some of the most impoverished
neighbourhoods. She left Bertrand and works and

lives alone. She decided that in fact she was happiest in her solitary state with her art, and nothing and no one should take that away from her.

About the author

Olivia King has been writing fiction and telling stories for as long as she can remember. She has enjoyed every moment of her writing journey. This is her third book of short stories. She also creates art and has included some pieces in this book. She hopes you enjoy the art and the stories. Smile.

Printed in Great Britain
by Amazon